This book belongs to

_____

_____

This edition published by Parragon Books Ltd in 2016

Parragon Books Ltd
Chartist House
15–17 Trim Street
Bath BA1 1HA, UK
www.parragon.com

ISBN 978-1-4748-4079-8

Printed in China

DISNEY MOVIE COLLECTION
A SPECIAL DISNEY STORYBOOK SERIES

Aladdin

PaRragon
Bath • New York • Cologne • Melbourne • Delhi
Hong Kong • Shenzhen • Singapore • Amsterdam

Deep in the Arabian desert, an evil
sorcerer named Jafar touched two halves
of a magical scarab together. Glowing, the
scarab flew across the desert. Where it
stopped, an immense tiger head formed
from the sand. This was the entrance
to the Cave of Wonders.

Afraid to enter the cave himself, Jafar ordered a thief named Gazeem to do it for him. Jafar was desperate to get his hands on the magical lamp. But as Gazeem stepped inside, a mystical voice boomed from the cave: "Only one may enter – a diamond in the rough!" Then the head sank into the sand, taking Gazeem with it.

"I must find this diamond in the rough," said Jafar.

Early the next morning, in the marketplace of
Agrabah, a poor young man named Aladdin took a
loaf of bread.

"Stop, street rat!" shouted the Sultan's guards.

Aladdin and his pet monkey, Abu, fled over rooftops
and balconies, up steps and down alleyways.

Outwitted, the guards gave up. Aladdin and Abu hurried back to their rooftop home.

Aladdin gazed at the Sultan's palace. "One day we'll be rich, live in a palace and never have any problems," he promised Abu. Then, they would never again have to steal in order to survive.

But Aladdin was wrong. In the palace, Princess
Jasmine had her own problems. The kingdom said she
had to marry a prince by her 18th birthday – in only
three days! But Jasmine wanted to marry for love.

Her father, the Sultan, didn't understand. But her
pet tiger, Rajah, did.

Jasmine's refusal to choose a husband upset the Sultan. Jafar, who was also the Sultan's advisor, convinced the Sultan he could help. But all he really wanted was the Sultan's blue diamond ring which would assist him in finding the 'diamond in the rough' the cave had mentioned.

He hypnotized the Sultan, just long enough to get the ring.

While Jafar plotted and planned, Jasmine disguised herself as a commoner and hugged Rajah goodbye. She had decided that it would be better to leave home than be forced to marry.

"I'll miss you," she said. "But I can't stay here and have my life lived for me. I want to see more of the world then this palace."

She climbed over the palace walls and was gone.

Having never been out of the palace, Jasmine loved Agrabah's bustling marketplace. She saw a hungry boy and took an apple from a fruit stand to give to him. She had never had to pay for things before so she didn't realize she was stealing.

"Thief!" shouted the vendor. Just then, Aladdin appeared and defended Jasmine. Quickly, he led her away.

Meanwhile, in his secret chamber, Jafar used the
Sultan's diamond to activate the Sands of Time.
    "Show me the diamond in the rough – he
commanded the magical hourglass.
    The sands showed him Aladdin!
    Jafar ordered the palace guards
to bring him to the palace.

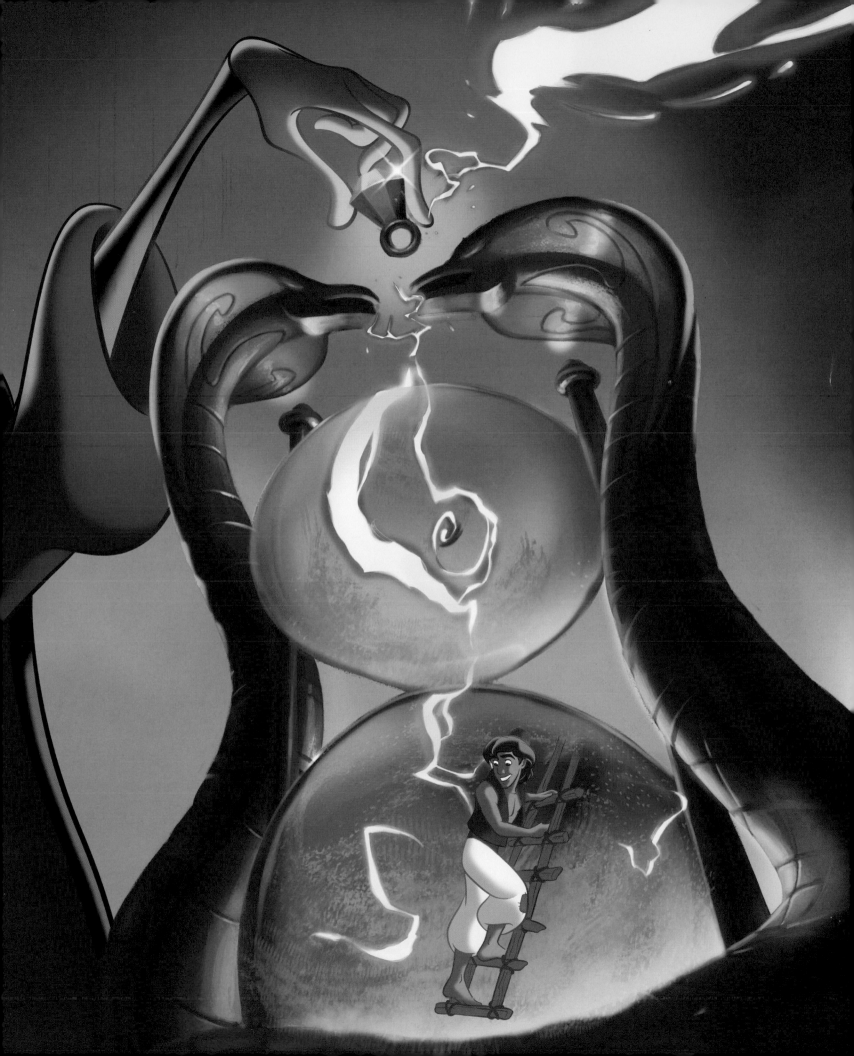

Aladdin took Jasmine to his home, a ragged shelter on the roof of a building. Jasmine thought he was clever and handsome. Aladdin thought she was beautiful.

"Where are you from?" he asked.

"It doesn't matter." she replied. "I ran away and I am not going back."

Suddenly, the palace guards thundered up the stairs and grabbed Aladdin.

Jasmine threw off her scarf. "Unhand him, by order of the Princess!" she ordered.

"I would," said the captain, shocked to see the princess, "but my orders come from Jafar."

The guards threw Aladdin and Abu in a dungeon.
Aladdin thought sadly about Jasmine. She was a princess!
No matter how much he liked her, she could never love a
poor boy like him.
Suddenly, an old prisoner stepped out from the shadows.

He offered to make Aladdin rich – if Aladdin would do one small errand for him. The old man opened a secret passage out of the dungeon. They could now escape.

The old man wanted Aladdin to retrieve a
magical item for him, an old magical lamp. He led
Aladdin and Abu to the mysterious tiger's head –
the Cave of Wonders.

"Who disturbs my slumber?" A voice roared as
Aladdin approached.

"It is I," said Aladdin.

"Proceed," thundered the voice.

"Bring me the lamp!" the old man called.

"Touch nothing but the lamp," the voice warned as Aladdin and Abu walked down the steep steps into a huge treasure chamber. A magic carpet playfully tugged at Abu from behind a pile of gold.

"Maybe you can help us," Aladdin said to the carpet. "We're trying to find a lamp."

The carpet led Aladdin to a lake deep in the cave. In its centre was a huge altar of rocks with a lamp on top. Aladdin crossed the lake and scrambled up the rocks. The lamp looked old and battered – worthless.

Just then, Abu saw a statue holding a glowing gem. He had to have it!

"Abu! No!" Aladdin shouted from the top of the stairs as Abu grabbed for the gem.

Even the Carpet tried to stop him. But it was too late.

"You have touched forbidden treasures!" The tiger's voice thundered.

The ground rumbled and shook. Aladdin was flung into the air. The cave floor turned to molten lava. Catching Aladdin and Abu, the Carpet soared for the cave entrance. But Aladdin fell off!

Frantically, Aladdin grabbed for the old man's hand on the crumbling stairs. Aladdin begged him for help.

"Give me the lamp!" the man said, revealing a dagger. Then SNAP! Abu bit the man's hand. The old man pulled away and Aladdin and Abu tumbled back into the cave.

The old man laughed as he took off his beard. It was actually Jafar in disguise. He reached inside his cloak for the lamp, howling in despair once he realized it was gone.

Back in the cave, Abu pulled out the lamp.
He had deftly grabbed it back from Jafar!

Aladdin rubbed the lamp. Suddenly, sparks flew, smoke swirled and POOF – a genie appeared!

"You get three wishes." The Genie told Aladdin.

"You probably can't even get us out of this cave," Aladdin said skeptically.

"We're out of here!" The Genie shouted. In seconds, they were out of the cave – without using a single wish!

Aladdin still had all three wishes to use.

"Can you turn me into a prince?" he asked the Genie.

The Genie looked at Aladdin's size and build. He measured here ... and there ...

And then ... with a wave of his big blue hands – Presto!
The Genie dressed Aladdin in clothes fit for a prince.
"We'll call you Prince Ali Abawa," the Genie announced.

"Hang onto your turban!"
the Genie shouted. Suddenly,
acrobats, dancers, sword-twirlers
and a menagerie of animals
appeared. Aladdin rode into
Agrabah in a spectacular parade!

Arriving at the palace, Aladdin asked for Jasmine's hand. The Sultan was impressed.

But Jasmine wasn't. "I am not some prize to be won!" She stormed away.

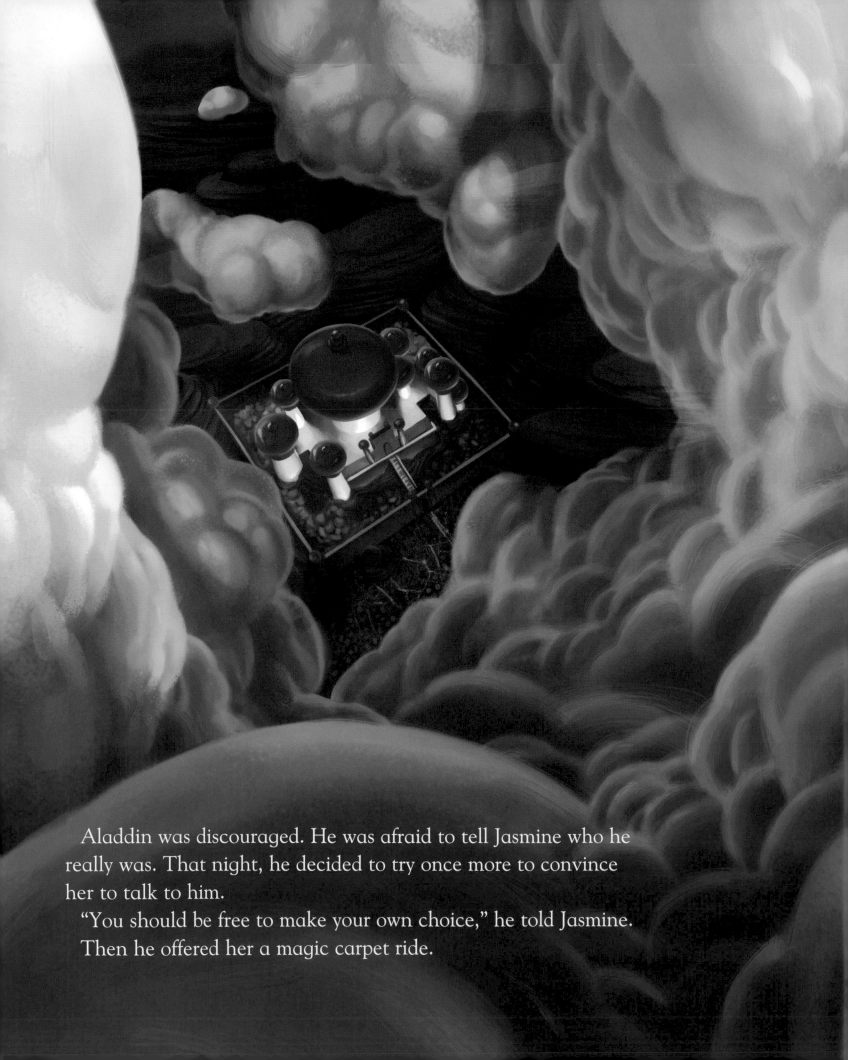

Aladdin was discouraged. He was afraid to tell Jasmine who he really was. That night, he decided to try once more to convince her to talk to him.

"You should be free to make your own choice," he told Jasmine. Then he offered her a magic carpet ride.

Together, Aladdin and Jasmine flew through the starry night, over deserts, mountains and seas, past cities and countrysides, discovering a whole new world – and each other. She quickly realized he was the boy from the market.

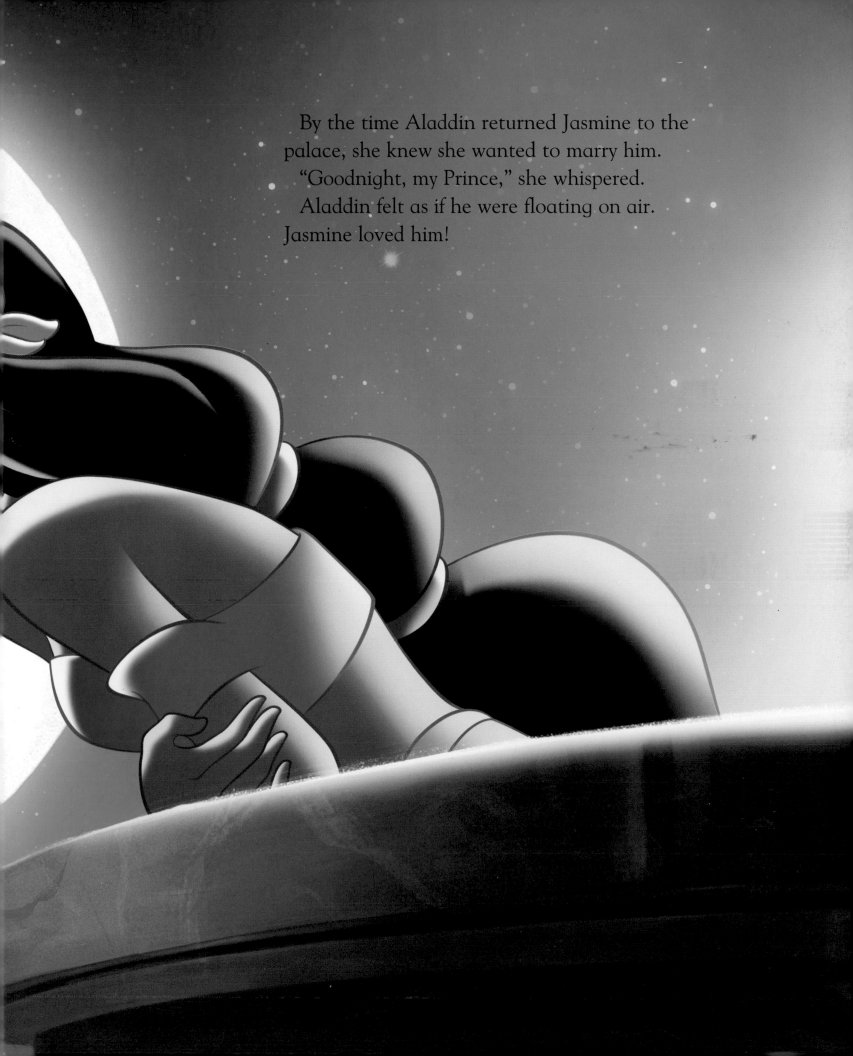

By the time Aladdin returned Jasmine to the
palace, she knew she wanted to marry him.
"Goodnight, my Prince," she whispered.
Aladdin felt as if he were floating on air.
Jasmine loved him!

But Jafar had evil plans for Aladdin.
"You've worn out your welcome, Prince Abooboo,"
Jafar said. He ordered guards to bind and gag Aladdin
and throw him into the sea! Aladdin used his second
wish to get the Genie to rescue him.

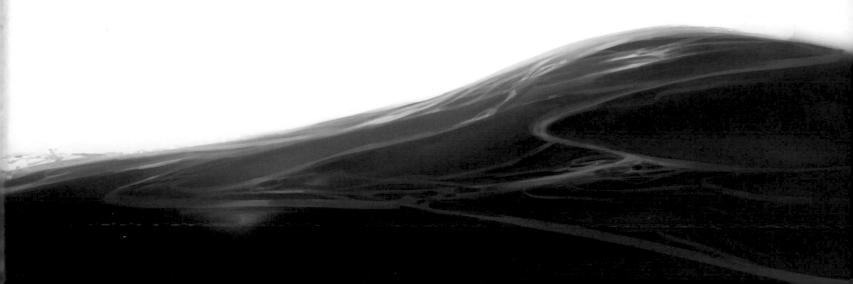

At the palace, Jafar hypnotized the Sultan again. "Tell Jasmine she must marry me," he ordered. Suddenly, Aladdin entered the room and ruined Jafar's evil plan. Jafar was furious.

But Jafar knew where Aladdin kept the lamp. He sent his parrot, Iago, to steal it.

When Jafar rubbed the
lamp, the Genie appeared.
"I wish to rule as the
Sultan," Jafar thundered.

The Genie had to obey. He transformed Jafar into the Sultan. Then, he lifted the palace into the air. With his magic staff, Jafar banished Aladdin and Abu to a frozen wasteland.

Luckily, the Magic Carpet found them and carried them back to the palace.

Meanwhile, things looked hopeless for Jasmine and the
Sultan. Suddenly, Aladdin appeared. Quickly, she pretended
to flirt with the vain sorcerer. She had to try and distract Jafar
long enough for Aladdin to save her and her father!

Aladdin hurled himself at Jafar. The wicked sorcerer used his magic to surround himself and the lamp with flames and swords. He changed the Sultan into a puppet and Abu into a toy. He imprisoned Jasmine in a giant hourglass. He even transformed himself into a giant cobra!

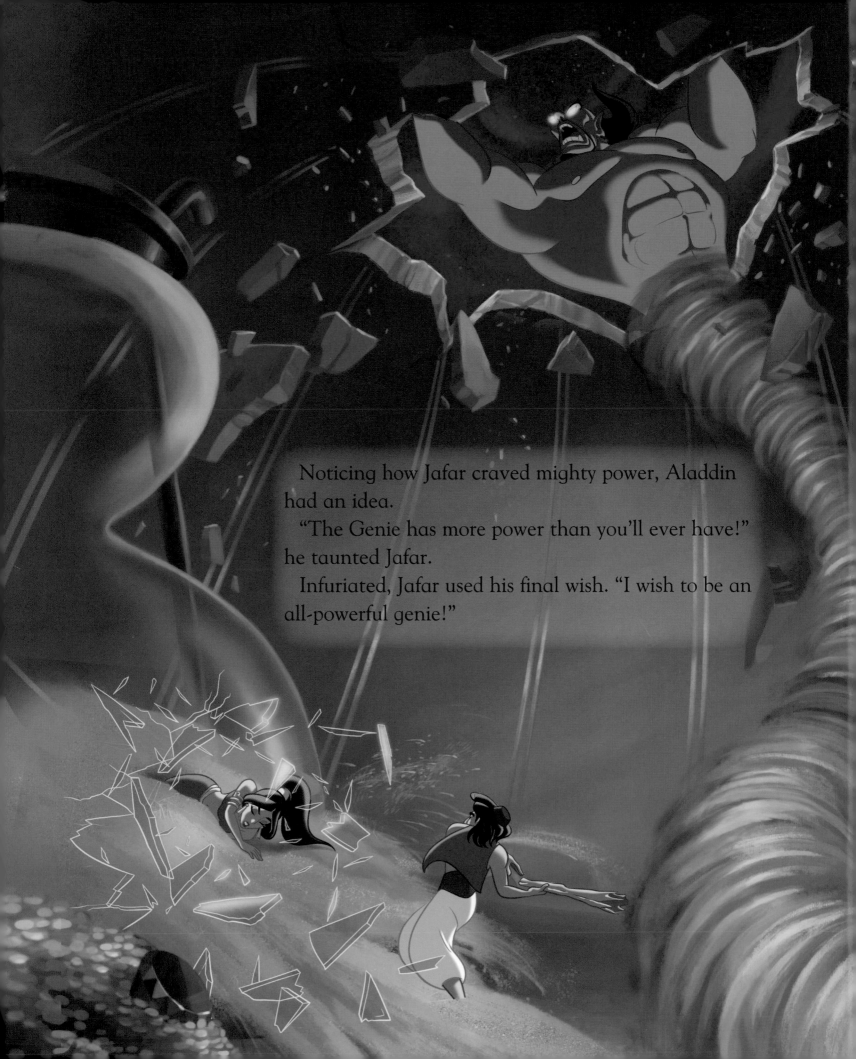

Noticing how Jafar craved mighty power, Aladdin
had an idea.

"The Genie has more power than you'll ever have!"
he taunted Jafar.

Infuriated, Jafar used his final wish. "I wish to be an
all-powerful genie!"

Jafar was transformed into a genie. But he had forgotten that although powerful, genies were doomed to live in a lamp and obey their master's wishes.

Aladdin picked up the lamp – and imprisoned Jafar inside. He was trapped forever.

As a reward for Aladdin's bravery, the Sultan changed the law so Jasmine could marry whomever she chose. Of course, she chose Aladdin.

Aladdin used his third wish to keep his promise and free the Genie. Sadly, Aladdin and the Genie said goodbye, but they knew they would be friends forever.